FEB 2001

You'll Soon Grow into Them, Titch

Pat Hutchins
You'll Soon Grow

into Them, Titch

A Mulberry Paperback Book  New York

Library of Congress Cataloging in Publication Data

Hutchins, Pat (date)
You'll soon grow into them, Titch.
Summary: The tables turn at last for Titch, who has
been inheriting his older siblings' outgrown clothes.
[1. Brothers and sisters—Fiction.
2. Clothing and dress—Fiction.] I. Title.
PZ7.H96165Yo 1983 [E] 82-11755
ISBN 0-688-11507-1

FOR AMY

Titch needed new pants.

His brother Pete said,
"You can have my old pants,
they're too small for me."

"They're still a bit big for me,"
said Titch.

"You'll soon grow into them,"
said Pete.

And when Titch needed a new sweater,

his sister Mary said,
"You can have my old sweater,
it's too small for me."

"It's still a bit big for me,"
said Titch.

"You'll soon grow into it,"
said Mary.

And when Titch needed new socks,

they both said,
"You can have our old socks,
they're too small for us."

"And I'll soon grow into them,"
said Titch.

So Dad and Titch went shopping.

They bought a brand-new pair of pants,

a brand-new sweater,

and a brand-new pair of socks.

And when Mother brought
their brand-new baby home,
Titch wore the new clothes.

"There," said Titch,
"he can have my old pants,

and my old sweater,

and my old socks.
They're much too small for me!"

"They're a bit big for him,"
said Pete and Mary.

"He'll soon grow into them,"
said Titch.